Winston of Churchill

One Bear's Battle
Against Global Warming

JEAN DAVIES OKIMOTO

Illustrated by JEREMIAH TRAMMELL

SASQUATCH BOOKS
SEATTLE

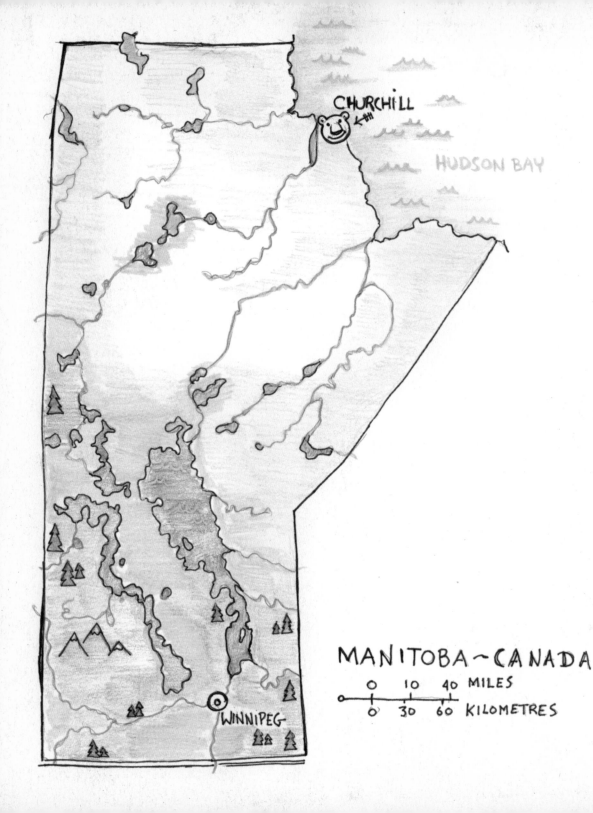

CHURCHILL

HUDSON BAY

MANITOBA ~ CANADA

0   10   40 MILES

0   30   60 KILOMETRES

WINNIPEG

For Sarah, Nina, Joe, Naomi, Lily and Hana
JDO

For Mom and Dad
JT

Published by Jean Davies Okimoto/Sasquatch Books
Printed in China
Distributed by PGW/Perseus
15 14 13 12 11 10 09 08 07   9 8 7 6 5 4 3 2 1

Cover and interior design: Elizabeth Cromwell/Books in Flight
Library of Congress Control Number: 2007931109
ISBN-10: 1-57061-543-8
ISBN-13: 978-157061-543-6

Sasquatch Books
119 South Main Street, Suite 400
Seattle, WA 98104
(206) 467-4300
www.sasquatchbooks.com
custserv@sasquatchbooks.com

♲ Printed on 100% post-consumer waste recycled paper

Winston of Churchill was a great white bear. Every year in the late fall and early winter, Winston and the other polar bears came to hunt from the ice of Hudson Bay near the town of Churchill, in the Canadian province of Manitoba.

Winston was a fierce, brave bear,

and when Winston spoke, every bear listened.

Young and old bears, father bears, mother bears, teenager bears, all the bears listened. Even cubs. Every furry face was turned to Winston and a hush fell over the crowd.

"My fellow creatures, I have called this meeting today to discuss a serious problem."

"The ice is melting. We are losing our home. The time has come for action.
This is no time for ease and comfort. It is the time to dare and endure."

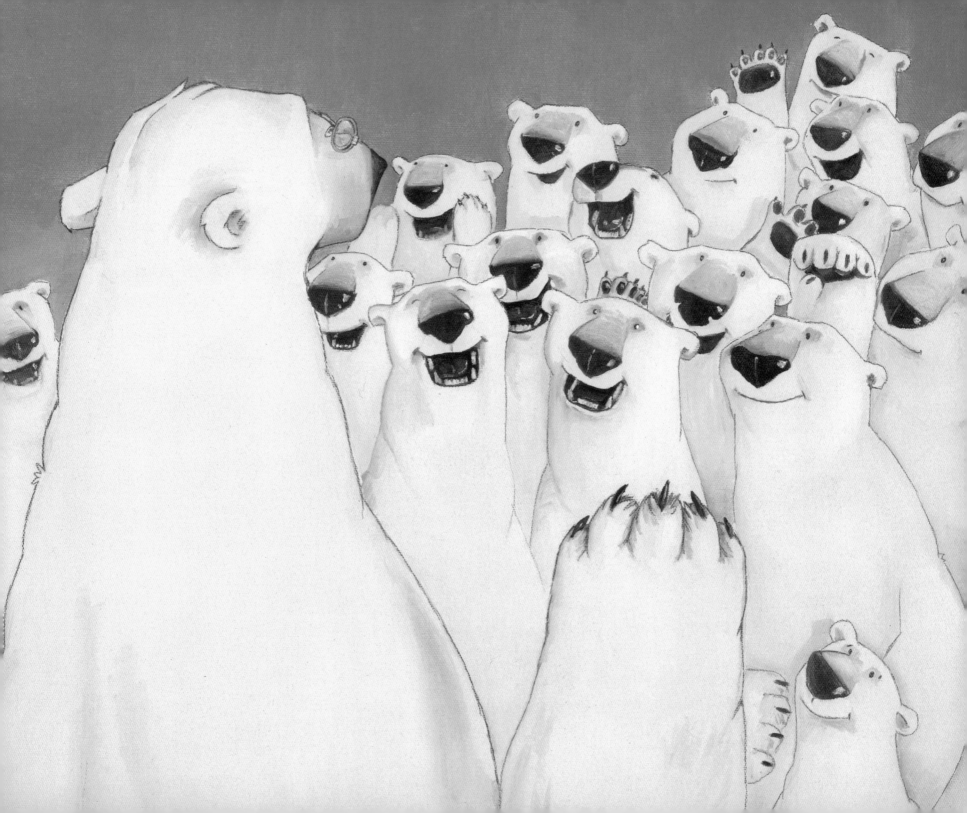

"Do we want to spend the rest of our lives at the dump?"
"No! No!" shouted the bears. "We want ice! Ice is nice!"

"We will fight for ice," boomed Winston. "We shall defend our island, whatever the cost may be. We shall fight on the beaches. We shall fight on the landing grounds. We shall fight in the fields and in the streets. We shall fight on the hills. We shall never surrender."

All the bears cheered and cheered.

In the back row a cub raised his paw.
"Yes, son," Winston called on him.
"We don't live on an island. We live in Manitoba."
"I know that, it was just a figure of speech."

Winston noticed the cub raised his paw again. "Now what?"
"I have another question."
"What is it?" Winston puffed on his cigar.
"Who are we fighting?"

"I was about to get to that, son." Winston puffed again on his cigar. "Ice is melting because it's getting too warm around here and people are doing it with their cars and smoke stacks. And cutting down trees."

"How does that happen?"

"I wrote this book about it. There's one for everybody. Come up here and help me pass them out."

The earth has some gas around it that holds in the heat of the sun.
It's called the atmosphere.

If you get too much of some of these gases,
the heat near the earth gets stuck and the earth heats up.

WHY IT'S GETTING HOTTER

by
Winston of Churchill
Manitoba, Canada,
North America, Earth

Burning gasoline in cars makes carbon dioxide.

Methane gas comes from rotting garbage in landfills.

Digging for oil and natural gas and mining coal lets out a gas
called nitrous oxide. Too much of these gases is no good.

But green plants turn carbon dioxide into oxygen,
which is very good.

People need to burn less gas, make less garbage, and
plant more trees.

"But what can we do?"

"We can't do anything," Winston said. "We are bears.
We don't drive cars or burn coal. We like it cold."

"Yes, ice is nice," everyone agreed.

"It's the people who have to change," shouted Winston.
"Not bears! And we must convince them to do it!"

POLAR BEAR
ALERT

STOP
DONT WALK
IN THIS AREA

"Now listen carefully, here's my plan: tomorrow when
the tourists board the tundra buggies and those buggies
begin to roll, they'll roll right into our polar bear protest!
Are you with me? Are you ready to march?"

"Yes!" shouted the bears.

"Are you ready to fight for ice?"

"Yes!" shouted the bears.

But one bear didn't say yes.
One bear said, "No."
Everyone looked to see who it was.

The bear who said "no" said it again.
"No."
It was Winston's wife.

Winston and his wife left the group to have a private talk.

"This is very embarrassing," Winston said to his wife. "Why did you say no?"

"I'm not going on the march, Winston, unless you quit smoking that thing. You're polluting the air, and that makes it hotter here. That thing in your mouth is an instrument of pollution."

"Sometimes a cigar is a cigar," growled Winston.

"How can you convince people to stop doing what they're doing unless you can show that every little bit helps?" His wife glared at him. "No cigar or I'm not going."

The next morning it was cold and clear, and in the town of Churchill the tourists began to wake up.

They ate breakfast in the restaurants of the town.

Then it was time to go. Time to see the bears.
The tourists were very excited as they boarded the tundra buggies.

There were people from Billings, Montana; Tacoma, Washington; Portland,
Oregon; and Brunswick, Maine.

There were people from Evanston, Illinois; Hudson, Ohio; Boise, Idaho; and
Halifax, Nova Scotia.

There was even a family from Tokyo, Japan; three couples from Auckland,
New Zealand; a man from San Diego, California; and two Welsh ladies who lived
in a place called Brynhyfryd Llanddarog that no one could pronounce.

They drove and drove but there was not a bear in sight.

The tourists kept staring out the windows at the tundra, looking for the bears, but the only thing they saw was tundra. The tourists were very disappointed. They began to grumble and complain. One man from Boise wanted his money back. So did a lady from Billings.

Their complaints got louder and louder, when suddenly, far out on the tundra there was an amazing sight.

Every bear in Churchill was marching across the tundra.
They were following a fierce, brave bear.

And the fierce, brave bear they were following . . . was chewing a twig.

"Save our home! It's up to you. We can all do our part," shouted Winston of
Churchill. "No matter how small. I have nothing to offer but blood, toil, tears and
sweat. But I say to you: Never, never, never give up."

The tourists were so excited to see the bears.
They took picture after picture,

and when they got home they showed
their pictures to their friends and families.

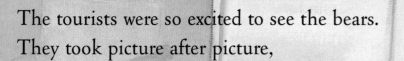

churchill

canada

WE
MUST ALL DO
OUR PART,
NO MATTER
HOW SMALL

winston

In every picture was a fierce, brave bear holding a sign
that said, "We must all do our part, no matter how small."

And the bear was chewing a twig.

THE PLIGHT OF THE POLAR BEARS . . .
AND WHERE WINSTON GOT HIS NAME

Because the earth is getting warmer, the ice in Hudson Bay breaks up earlier and the polar bears don't have as much time to hunt for their food. The bears have become thinner and female bears are having fewer cubs, some of which don't survive. Polar bears typically swim from one patch of sea ice to another to hunt for food. But as the melting ice makes the distances greater between the patches, the bears must swim farther and farther distances. This is very hard on them and scientists have said that some of the bears have actually drowned.

Winston the polar bear is named for a real person, one of the greatest leaders in history, Sir Winston Churchill. He was the courageous prime minister of England during World War II and his words inspired the people to never give up in the war. He was the prime minister from 1940 until 1945. When Winston the polar bear is trying to lead the bears to protest global warming, he uses some of the famous words of Sir Winston Churchill.

Sir Winston Churchill was often seen with a cigar in his mouth (back then people didn't know the dangers of smoking) and with his hand raised high with two fingers making a "V for victory" sign, a sight that cheered the people and gave them hope. In addition to being a great leader, Sir Winston Churchill was also a painter and an author and in 1953 he won the Nobel Prize in Literature.

In this story, Winston the polar bear is an author, too. His book "Why It's Getting Hotter" is based on a real book called *Why Are the Ice Caps Melting? The Dangers of Global Warming* by Anne Rockwell, illustrated by Paul Meisel. It is part of the Let's-Read-and-Find-Out Science® series. This book gives many details about global warming and would be a very good one to read to learn more than the simple things Winston the bear wrote in his book. But even though Winston's book only has a few facts, Winston the polar bear has an idea that he hopes might save the home of the polar bears and help all the creatures of the earth: Everyone must do their part, no matter how small.